The Great Blue Grump

Story
Jill Creighton

Art
Kitty Macaulay

Annick Press • Toronto • New York

With love to Luke, and to Rob, as ever.
—J.C.

For Jenny.
—K.M.

WHAT IS THE GREAT BLUE GRUMP?

He's not a bird, like the bald eagle.

He's not a snake.

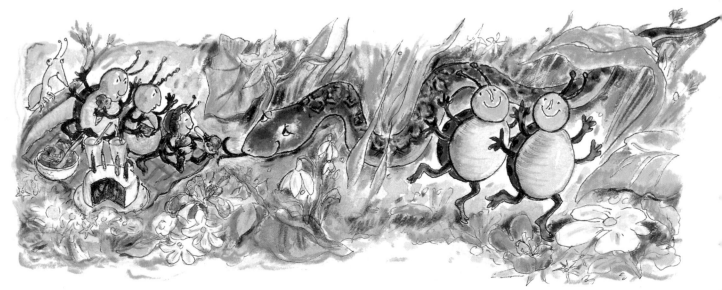

He stands up
straight
like a grizzly bear,
but he can crawl
 if he wants.

He never gets
 much sleep.

That's why
 he's grumpy.

How big is the Great Blue Grump?

He is
bigger than
a ring-tailed lemur,

but smaller than a mountain gorilla.

What does he look like?

*He has fluffy
brown hair,
sleepy brown eyes
and a furry face,
and he's covered in blue.*

Where is the Great Blue Grump?

He is not in the rainforest
like the three-toed sloth,

...nor in the desert like the frilled lizard.

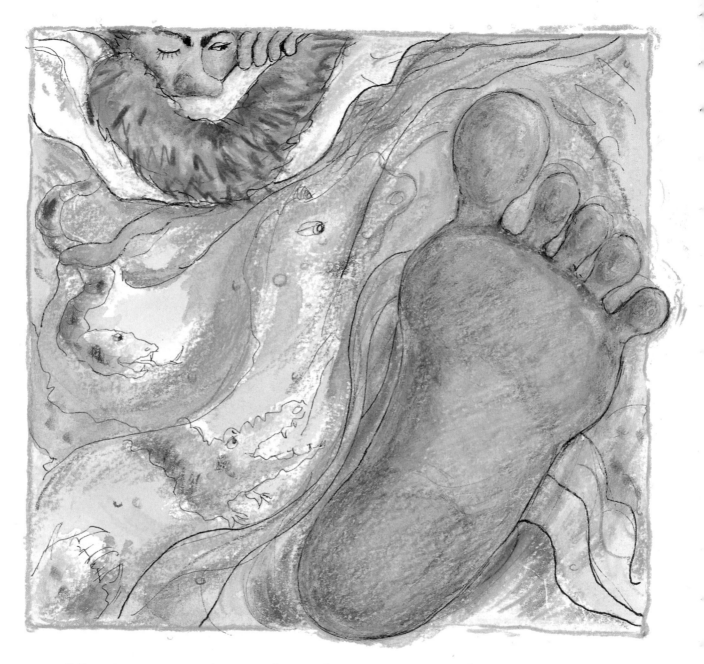

He is upstairs, sleeping on my father's bed.

What

does he eat?

The Great Blue Grump eats everything...

strawberries, meat, chocolate, bean sprouts.

But he **doesn't** like

asparagus.

Can he make a sound?

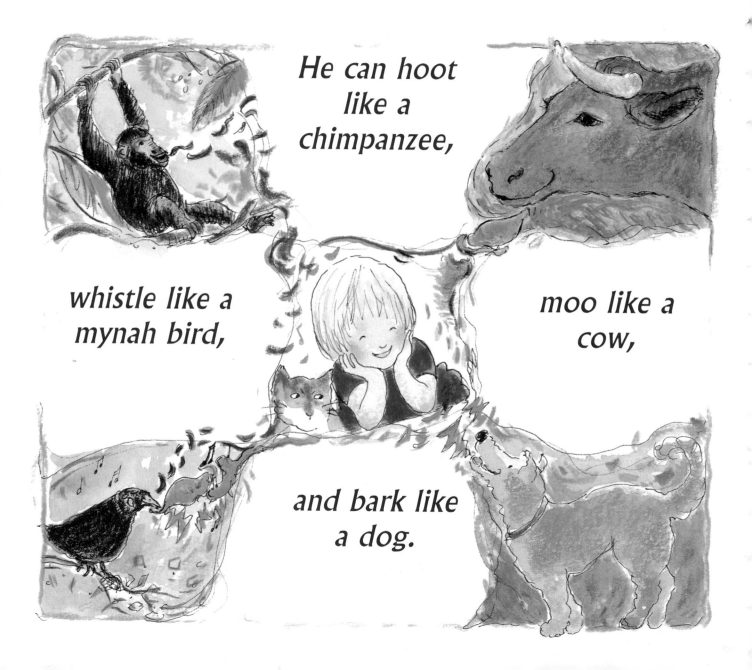

He can hoot like a chimpanzee,

moo like a cow,

whistle like a mynah bird,

and bark like a dog.

But mostly you will hear him SNORT, snuffle,
sigh, and GRUNT
as he settles down to sleep
through the morning.

What does he do, the Great Blue Grump?

He will never eat you for dinner
like a tiger would.

He will never take up too much room
and squash you flat as a pancake
like an elephant would.

But he can get you in his grip...

He can squeeze you up tight.

He can tickle your cheek with his
bristly whiskers,

and tickle your ribs
with his powerful fingers.

Can I see him?

Let's go look.

Yay! He woke up!

I just love the Great Blue Grump.

He's the best dad in the world.

Annick Press Ltd.

Annick Press gratefully acknowledges the support of the
Canada Council and the Ontario Arts Council.

Canadian Cataloguing in Publication Data

Creighton, Jill
  The great blue grump
ISBN 1-55037-432-X (pbk.) ISBN 1-55037-433-8 (bound)

I. Macaulay, Kitty. II. Title.

PS8555.R443G73 1997   jC813'.54   C96-990068-6
PZ7.C73Gr 1997

The art in this book was rendered in pen and ink and coloured pencil.
The text was typeset in Flareserif 821.

Distributed in Canada by:
Firefly Books Ltd.
3680 Victoria Park Avenue
Willowdale, ON
M2H 3K1

Published in the U.S.A. by Annick Press (U.S.) Ltd.
Distributed in the U.S.A. by:
Firefly Books (U.S.) Inc.
P.O. Box 1338
Ellicott Station
Buffalo, NY 14205

Printed and bound in Canada by Friesens.